This
MOUSE ❀ WORKS
Classics Collection Storybook

belongs to

allison G.

THE ARISTOCATS

© The Walt Disney Company
Printed in the United States of America
ISBN: 1-57082-446-0
10 9 8 7 6 5 4 3

Not very long ago, at the turn of the century, there were no automobiles on the streets of Paris. Pedestrians took leisurely walks through the city, and the very rich, elegantly clad in the latest fashions, went out in their sumptuous carriages for promenades.

Madame Adelaide Bonfamille was a charming elderly lady, and she was very rich. She often took her four cats out in her carriage for fresh air and a tour of the city. Madame was so fond of her cats that she thought of them as her children.

Duchess was a beautiful white angora cat, and Berlioz, Toulouse, and Marie were her three very talented kittens. Berlioz aspired to be a composer; Toulouse, a famous painter; and Marie, a prima donna. They all loved Madame dearly. She was a very kind woman.

Madame Bonfamille was very proud of her adopted children, but Edgar, her butler, was not so fond of them.

"Now look at that Berlioz!" he muttered under his breath when they reached home that morning. "He jumps on top of Frou-Frou the mare and Madame does not say a word about it. She spoils them!"

Madame encouraged the kittens to pursue their talents, even when they turned her home all topsy-turvy.

As soon as he entered the house, Berlioz made a dash for Madame's ball of red wool. *Swish!* It unravelled across the room.

"My little darlings have so much fun!" Madame thought. She looked over to Toulouse who was at his easel starting a painting. "Good work, Toulouse!" she said to the proud kitten. When Roquefort the mouse came out of his hole to play and grabbed hold of Berlioz's tail for a ride, she smiled. "Hello, Roquefort! Are you out for a walk?" she said.

Madame liked Roquefort. He was a very friendly mouse. Roquefort loved Madame and the cats because they never tried to chase him away.

Everyone was very happy in Madame Bonfamille's home except the grumpy Edgar. He was perhaps over-proud of his position as butler, and felt it was beneath him to play babysitter for four spoiled and very silly cats. "I am not a butler," he would often think to himself, "but a catsitter for four animals who think they are Aristocats!"

Berlioz soon lost interest in the ball of red wool and went to the piano, his favorite musical instrument.

Marie joined him, and to his virtuoso playing she sang, "Do, re, mi, fa, sol, la, ti, do! Ow, ow, ow, ow, ow, ow, ow, meow!"

Duchess sat on a velvet-cushioned armchair nearby and listened to her daughter sing and her son play.

"Marie will become a famous prima donna," she thought with a smile. "And Berlioz will give piano recitals all over the world!" Duchess was very grateful to Madame Bonfamille for her kindness and generosity. "We will always live here with her," she thought happily.

All of a sudden, the doorbell rang and startled
everyone. Berlioz, Toulouse, and Marie were
Aristocats, but they were also very curious kittens.
They ran to the front door to see who had come.

It was Mr. Georges Hautecourt, Madame
Bonfamille's attorney. Berlioz waved his paw at the
old gentleman. The kittens were very fond of him.

"Madame is upstairs in her salon, sir," said Edgar.
"Please follow me."

But Mr. Hautecourt was very old and suffered from arthritis. The old man could not climb the stairs. Edgar had to carry him on his back to Madame's salon!

"Oh, thank you. Thank you so very much," said the attorney when they reached the salon. When the door closed behind the old man, Edgar almost collapsed!

"What an exhausting man!" he muttered.

Madame, with her precious Duchess in her arms, welcomed her life-long friend.

"My dear, dear friend," she said, "I am so grateful that you should come at such short notice."

"It is my pleasure, my dearest Adelaide!" he said respectfully. He then stood up as straight as he could and bent over to kiss Madame's hand. Instead, he took hold of Duchess' furry white tail and kissed that! Madame Bonfamille giggled at her friend's mistake. Mr. Hautecourt turned red.

Meanwhile, Edgar had slipped into the room next door. The clever butler had guessed that Mr. Hautecourt's unexpected visit had to do with money... Madame's very large fortune. Edgar carefully listened to their conversation through the pipes. Madame Bonfamille did not have an heir. Edgar hoped that she would reward him in her will for his many years of loyalty and good service. He hoped to inherit her money.

"My dear Mr. Hautecourt," he overheard her tell the old man, "I have carefully thought about my situation and have found a solution which would make me very happy. I would like to leave my home and my fortune to my darling cats! They have made me so happy, and I am sure Edgar will be glad to look after them when I am gone."

Edgar thought that he would faint. The color drained from his face and his smile vanished. "She will leave everything to those cats and not a thing to me!" he thought with fury. "I won't have it! The cats must go!"

Edgar quickly went to the kitchen. Carefully he prepared the cats' dinner. He mixed their milk with breadcrumbs and a little honey and then added a few sleeping pills to the mixture.

"They will fall asleep and then I will take them far away and leave them there," he thought to himself with pleasure. "And Madame Bonfamille will have to leave her fortune to me – and only me!"

"Dinner's ready!" called Edgar to the cats. They all came running, and very soon the four hungry cats were lapping up their meal. Roquefort joined them and Duchess let him share her food. Edgar always prepared good dinners.

"Isn't this delicious!" asked Edgar with a crooked smile. "Edgar's special recipe for cats! You won't find anything like it in all of Paris."

As soon as the cats finished eating they started to feel very sleepy. They slowly crawled to their basket. Roquefort returned to his hole, where he fell sound asleep.

"They are exhausted!" thought Madame Bonfamille when she found her cats sleeping peacefully.

Edgar was thinking very different thoughts. "Good work!" he whispered to himself with a snicker. "Sweet dreams, my little cats!"

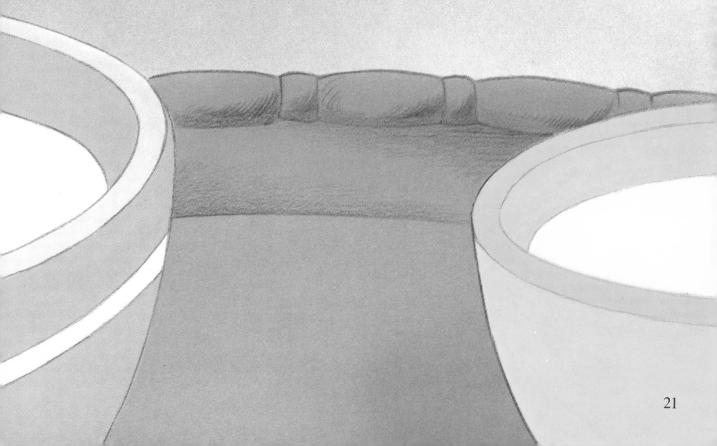

After Madame Bonfamille had gone to bed, Edgar slipped out of the house with the cats in their basket. He placed them in the sidecar of his motorcycle and drove out to the country.

"I will leave them beneath a bridge," he mused. "They will have fresh air, a roof over their heads, and water to drink! Country life will be excellent for their health!"

Everything was working out very well, and Edgar was so pleased that he did not see Napoleon and Lafayette, the two guard dogs of a nearby farm. Napoleon and Lafayette did not like loud motorcycles, nor did they like the smug look on Edgar's face.

"Let's chase this fellow off the road," suggested Napoleon.

"Okay, Napoleon. I wouldn't mind some fun," agreed Lafayette.

"Ready!" barked Napoleon.

"Ready!" growled Lafayette.

The two dogs took off after Edgar on his motorcycle, barking furiously. They took Edgar completely by surprise. He tried to speed away, but the dogs were professional motorcycle chasers. While Lafayette blocked the way, Napoleon snapped at Edgar's ankles.

With a scream, Edgar skidded off the road and zipped down the riverbank by the bridge, with Napoleon and Lafayette right on his tail. He hit a bump and the basket with the cats flew up in the air, landing safely in the reeds by the river.

Edgar's troubles were not over. He sped across the
river and up the other bank, followed by Napoleon and
Lafayette. The two dogs were enjoying the chase too
much to let him go. Snarls, barks, growls, and howls
followed the evil butler down the road.

When they caught up with him, Lafayette took a bite
out of his pants and Napoleon jumped into the sidecar.
Edgar swung at him with his umbrella, but the dog
would not jump out. Edgar had no choice but to kick
the sidecar off the motorcycle. Quickly he sped away
to the safety of the streets of Paris.

Meanwhile, by the riverbank, four frightened pairs of eyes searched the unfamiliar darkness. Duchess and her three kittens had awakened. They stepped out of their basket when the dogs' barking stopped.

"Mom, where are we?" asked Marie, terrified. Duchess did not answer. She did not know.

In Paris, Madame Bonfamille woke up. When she
saw that her cats' basket had disappeared, she searched
the whole house.

"Duchess! Toulouse! Marie! Berlioz! Where are
you?" she called. She rang for Edgar, but he, too, was
nowhere to be found.

Roquefort woke up to Madame's desperate calling for her cats. He was still sleepy, but he crawled out of his hole. Just then Edgar walked in the front door.

Madame ran downstairs when she heard the front door slam. "Edgar! Where were you? Somebody has stolen my children!" cried the distraught old lady.

"Stolen? I don't think so," lied Edgar. "They probably went out for a walk."

"But their basket is gone, too," protested Madame. "I know they were stolen."

Roquefort listened carefully. "Madame is right! Duchess, Berlioz, Toulouse, and Marie have been stolen!" thought the mouse with shock. "Oh! The milk we had for dinner made us sleepy! And Edgar just returned..." Slowly, the little mouse put two and two together. Edgar must have taken the cats away, but why? And where? Roquefort put on his detective cap and set out to get more evidence.

The next morning, Berlioz, Toulouse, and Marie were afraid. "What is going to happen to us?" they cried to their mother. "Where is Madame? We want to go home!"

Duchess did not know what to tell them. All of a sudden, an enormous tomcat jumped out in front of her.

"Hello! My name is Abraham de Lacy Giuseppe Tracy Thomas," he said. "O'Malley for short, and at your service, Ma'am."

O'Malley did not seem very distinguished, but Duchess decided to trust him. As best she could, she explained the strange happenings of the night before.

"I'm just an alley cat, Princess," he said to her with a smile. "But I'll do my best to get you back home!"

"He called me 'Princess'!" thought Duchess. "He knows we are Aristocats. I think he will get us back home."

But Marie was not so sure. "Mother, I don't want to follow him. He looks strange. Where will he take us?" she whimpered.

"He will take us back to Madame," said Duchess firmly. "O'Malley is going to help us get home. Now come on, do as you are told."

The tomcat had spotted a truck by the side of the road. Quietly he ordered them to jump into the back. Just as he leapt up into the truck after them, the engine roared and the truck pulled away, heading for Paris.

But a little farther ahead, the truck came again to a full stop. The driver let out a moan. A breakdown!

"Jump!" ordered O'Malley. If the driver found them in his truck, they would be in trouble.

O'Malley decided to follow the railroad tracks to the city. It was going to be a long walk, and Berlioz, Toulouse, and Marie were not very happy.

"We never should have taken that truck. We should have taken the train!" complained Berlioz.

"This cat doesn't look like the sort to take the train," commented Toulouse.

"Tell him that we are Aristocats!" said Marie, trying to look dignified.

"How ungrateful you are!" scolded Duchess. "You ought to thank him for helping us find our way home!"

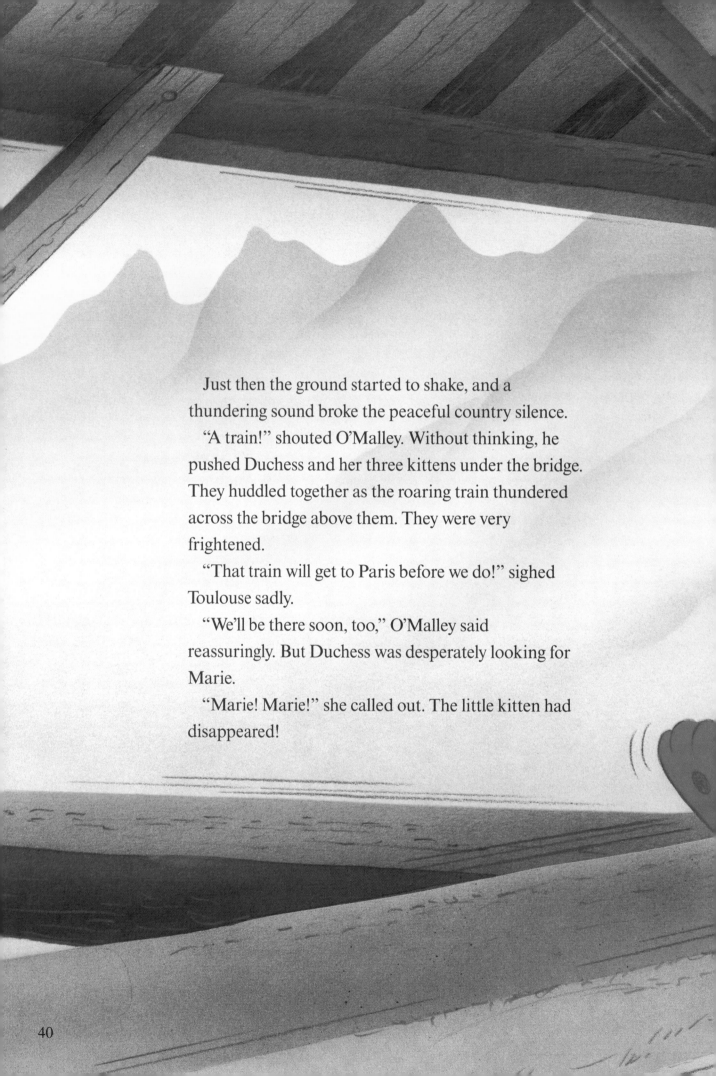

Just then the ground started to shake, and a
thundering sound broke the peaceful country silence.

"A train!" shouted O'Malley. Without thinking, he
pushed Duchess and her three kittens under the bridge.
They huddled together as the roaring train thundered
across the bridge above them. They were very
frightened.

"That train will get to Paris before we do!" sighed
Toulouse sadly.

"We'll be there soon, too," O'Malley said
reassuringly. But Duchess was desperately looking for
Marie.

"Marie! Marie!" she called out. The little kitten had
disappeared!

"Meow! Meow!" Two faint cries were heard below. When the train roared by, Marie had slipped off her perch and fallen into the river.

"Meow! Meow!" she cried as the current carried her away. O'Malley quickly jumped into the water to rescue her.

With a few powerful strokes, he reached Marie and,
lifting her above the water, he swam back to shore.
Duchess took hold of her daughter.

"O'Malley," she said with tears of gratitude in her
eyes, "I cannot thank you enough for this. You have
saved my daughter's life."

Marie looked up at the tomcat and shyly whispered a
little "Thank you." O'Malley had won her trust.

Two big white geese glided up to O'Malley. They had watched him rescue Marie.

"What a show you put on!" clucked the first.

"An excellent show!" added the second. "I thought cats hated to swim!"

"Who are you?" asked O'Malley, a little flattered.

"We are the Gabble Sisters. I am Emilie and she is Amelie," answered the first. "We are very pleased to meet you, Mr..."

"O'Malley," finished the tomcat. Emilie and Amelie giggled, much to the kittens' amusement.

Once everyone was safely back on the riverbank, the cats began to explain to the Gabble Sisters what had happened to them.

"Paris?" they interrupted, delighted. "We are going to Paris, as well! We've never been to the city! Why don't we all go together?"

Berlioz, Toulouse, and Marie had never seen geese before, and they were fascinated by Emilie and Amelie.

"Oh, yes! Come with us!" they cried out together. "We'd love you to come!" And with that, they all headed towards Paris.

It was close to midnight when they reached the city. O'Malley and the Aristocats said goodbye to the Gabble Sisters.

"Let's take a shortcut home," suggested O'Malley when the geese had left. "Hop on my back, Marie!" he called to the tired kitten. He then led them up to the rooftops, which he used as streets. Marie, Toulouse, and Berlioz had never seen the city from above.

"Wow! This is great!" exclaimed Toulouse.

They went by an open skylight. "Meeeow! Listen to that music!" cried Berlioz. "I've never heard anything like it!"

Why don't we stop?" offered O'Malley. "These musicians are good friends of mine."

They peered inside the skylight. The three little kittens could not believe their eyes.

Down below was a piano, a trumpet, a concertina, a contrabass, and a guitar. A group of cats was playing like crazy.

"What wonderful music!" cried Marie, who wanted to sing. "It's as exciting as the Opera!"

Duchess was a little taken aback. She was used to classical music.

"This is called "jazz," explained O'Malley. "It comes from America. These guys are great musicians. Let me introduce you."

"Oh, yes!" cried the kittens.

"This is Scat Cat, the famous trumpeter, and his band," said O'Malley. "Scat! These are my friends Duchess and her three kittens, Berlioz, Toulouse, and Marie!"

"Howdy!" said the Scat Cat, tipping his hat.

"It may not be Bach," said O'Malley to Duchess apologetically, "but it's a lot of fun. Would you like to dance?"

Shyly Duchess took his hand. She was soon whirling and jumping across the floor with the tomcat. Berlioz and Toulouse jumped on top of an old straw hat and danced just as hard. They had never had so much fun.

"This solo is for Duchess, the prettiest cat I have ever seen," announced Scat Cat. O'Malley was a little jealous, but Duchess was touched by the alley cat's melodious music.

When the music stopped, Berlioz blurted out, "I'm going to become a jazz musician, just like Scat Cat!"

"Wonderful!" said Scat, flattered. "I'll give you jazz lessons!"

"Oh, yeah!" purred the little kitten. Everyone chuckled.

"Time to move on," announced Scat Cat. "We always go for a tour of the streets at this hour. Nice meeting you!" he called to Duchess.

O'Malley and the Aristocats waved goodbye to their friends.

"Thank you!" Berlioz called after them.

"Thank you! Thank you!" echoed Toulouse and Marie. They'd had a grand time.

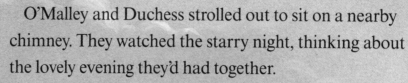

O'Malley and Duchess strolled out to sit on a nearby chimney. They watched the starry night, thinking about the lovely evening they'd had together.

Toulouse, Berlioz, and Marie gazed at them from the windowsill. They knew they would soon have to leave their new friend.

"Mother looks so happy, doesn't she?" said Marie sleepily.

"Yeah, and I love O'Malley! He has great friends!" added Berlioz with a yawn.

"It would be great if he could come and live with us," sighed Toulouse.

O'Malley was sad to see them go, too. "I'm going to miss you," he told Duchess.

"I'll miss you, too. You have been very nice to us, O'Malley. Thank you," said Duchess. "But we must go back to Madame."

Meanwhile, Edgar had returned to the countryside to retrieve his sidecar, hat, and umbrella. But Napoleon and Lafayette had made themselves at home with them. They were still laughing about their successful chase.

"This basket is very comfortable," Lafayette told Napoleon. "It's even got cushions! I wonder whose it was."

"Chasing that fellow was worth it," chuckled Napoleon, wearing his new hat. "These are better beds than our old haystack in the barn!"

Edgar sneaked up on them. He had brought his fishing pole to help him get his things back, but there was nothing he could do until the dogs had fallen asleep.

When Napoleon started to snore, Edgar gently lifted him out of the sidecar. He grabbed the hat in his teeth, and put the dog on the haystack. After he nabbed the umbrella, he slipped away. This time he had left his noisy motorcycle far down the road. He did not want to be chased again.

Back in Paris, Roquefort was conducting a thorough investigation. He had spent the day and the whole night interrogating all of the mice in the neighborhood.

Nobody had seen a thing. In the morning, he went to the stables to ask Frou-Frou the mare if she had noticed anything.

"Well, yes, Roquefort, I did notice something strange," said the mare. "The night before last, Edgar left on his motorcycle and came back *without* his sidecar. And last night he left again and came back *with* his sidecar!"

"Thank you, Frou-Frou. I've got a feeling Edgar is up to no good. Let me know if he goes out again," said the mouse.

When Roquefort returned to the house, he was very surprised to see that Duchess and the kittens had returned! They were saying goodbye to their friend when Edgar opened the door. The butler could not believe his eyes. How had they made it back? The cats did not even notice his surprise because they were so happy to be home. But Edgar quickly thought of a way to get rid of them ... forever.

"That's it! I will lock them up in a trunk and send them someplace far away!" he thought. "This time they won't ever come back!"

He grabbed a sack and caught the cats before they reached Madame's salon. The cats meowed and wriggled in the bag, trying to get free. Roquefort heard them and saw Edgar taking them out of the house.

"I knew Edgar was up to no good!" he said to himself. "I must get help. I'll go get that cat that brought them here. What was his name? O'Malley! That's it!"

Roquefort was courageous. He knew that cats did not like mice, especially alley cats, but he had to help his friends. He went after O'Malley. When he caught up with him, he explained what he had seen. O'Malley was furious. He did not like the idea that Duchess and the kittens might get hurt.

"Thanks, Roquefort. You're a brave mouse. I must rescue them before he hurts them, but we'll need help. Go find my friend Scat Cat and his band and tell them to meet me at Madame Bonfamille's house. Quick!" And with that, O'Malley ran back to the house.

Roquefort was a little nervous. Who was Scat Cat? Did he like mice?

When Roquefort found Scat Cat and his band, his heart was pounding furiously. How had the distinguished Duchess and the kittens met these cats? If he didn't quickly explain why he had come, they might just take a bite out of him. Scat Cat picked him up by the tail, while the Siamese cat poked at him.

"You say O'Malley sent you here?" Scat Cat asked the terrified mouse.

"Duchess and the kittens are in great danger," stammered Roquefort. "O'Malley needs you to help save them."

Scat Cat immediately let the mouse go. "Sure we'll help Duchess and her kittens. Show us the way," he ordered. They took off for Madame's house.

Edgar had taken the cats to the stables. He plopped them in a trunk and congratulated himself on his quick thinking.

"I'm scared!" cried Marie.

"I'm choking in here!" whined Toulouse. Berlioz said nothing, but his heart thumped loudly. Duchess tried to calm them. Just as Edgar closed the trunk, she heard Frou-Frou neighing. "We are in the stables," she realized.

"Frou-Frou! Help!" she cried as the lid closed.

Edgar was sticking a label on the trunk that read "Timbuktu, Africa."

Frou-Frou caught his coat in her mouth. The mare was furious. She pulled and pulled at Edgar's coat while the angry butler struggled to get free.

Frou-Frou wanted to kick him, but she couldn't get close enough. She held on to Edgar as long as she could, neighing for help. O'Malley heard her screams and ran into the stable just as Edgar's coat ripped free.

"That silly mare!" said Edgar. "She thinks she can stop me! I must get this trunk out in time for the pick-up." He pushed it towards the door.

Suddenly O'Malley jumped on top of him, hissing and growling. Edgar fought back, but had no idea who or what he was fighting. All he knew was that he was being scratched again and again. O'Malley fought hard. He would do anything for Duchess and the kittens.

All of a sudden Edgar was back on his feet. He grabbed a pitchfork and cornered O'Malley.

"I have you now!" the butler hissed. With one swift jab, he pinned the tomcat to the wall.

When Roquefort tiptoed up the pitchfork's handle and whispered to the cat, "Scat Cat and his friends are coming," O'Malley's face lit up. Edgar was not going to get away now.

The butler sighed. He was not enjoying this. Everything was getting much too difficult. He straightened out his clothes and pushed the trunk a little closer to the door.

"One, two, three, go!" a voice said, and suddenly what Edgar thought were one hundred cats jumped on him. They hissed, they bit, they scratched, they growled, and they pinned him down. Edgar could not move. Frou-Frou cheered them on. Roquefort held his breath. Duchess and the kittens were saved!

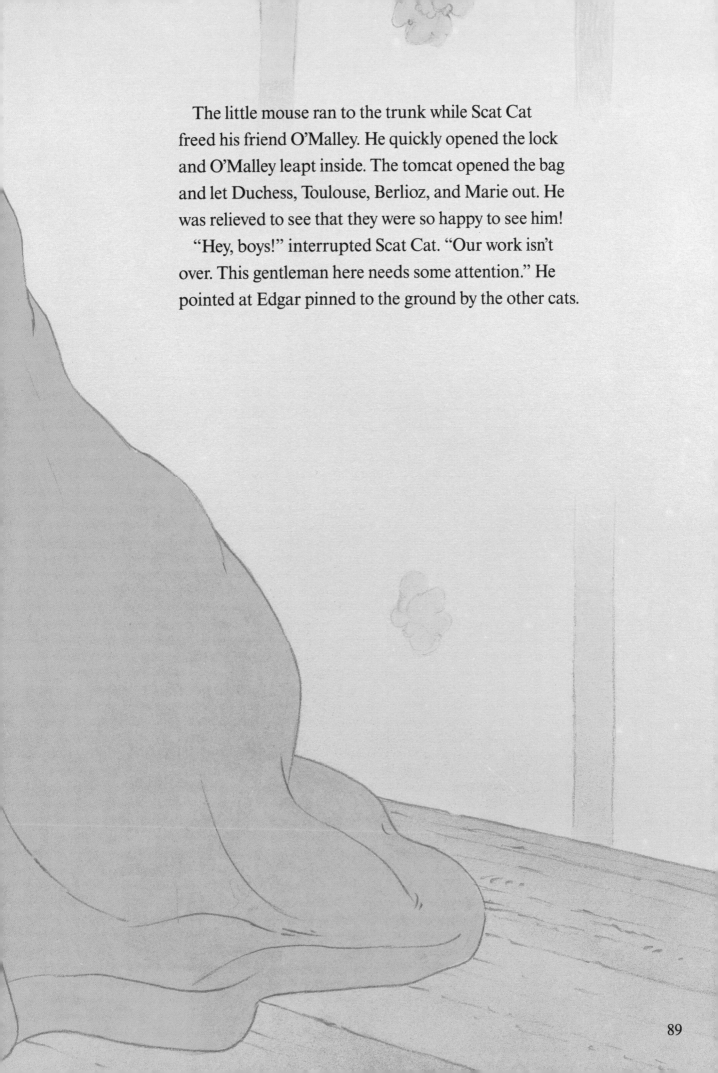

The little mouse ran to the trunk while Scat Cat
freed his friend O'Malley. He quickly opened the lock
and O'Malley leapt inside. The tomcat opened the bag
and let Duchess, Toulouse, Berlioz, and Marie out. He
was relieved to see that they were so happy to see him!

"Hey, boys!" interrupted Scat Cat. "Our work isn't
over. This gentleman here needs some attention." He
pointed at Edgar pinned to the ground by the other cats.

"Why don't we lock *him* up in the trunk and send *him* away?" proposed Frou-Frou. "That way, he'll never come back and bother us."

Everybody thought that Frou-Frou's idea was excellent. Edgar would be sent to Timbuktu! They tied him up, lifted him up with the help of a pulley, and Frou-Frou swiftly kicked him into the trunk. After they had locked it, they pushed the trunk outside to be hauled away by the moving company.

"He'll love those blue skies and palm trees in Timbuktu!" joked Scat Cat when the movers arrived to pick up the trunk.

"Bon voyage!" teased the Siamese cat. Everybody laughed. They happily watched the movers check the label and carry Edgar away.

Duchess and O'Malley said goodbye to Scat Cat and his band and thanked them for their help. They promised to come to the attic for another jazz evening soon.

Madame Bonfamille was very happy when she saw her cats. Tears and hugs and purrs and furry cuddles went out for everyone. Madame could see that Duchess was very fond of O'Malley. She asked him to stay.

With a bit of grooming, O'Malley the alley cat became Madame's fifth Aristocat. She adopted him and added him to her will. And when her five children posed for a photograph, what a handsome family they made!